The Rocking Horse

Karrie Loomis

D1367347

Copyright © 2014 by Karrie Loomis

All rights reserved.

ISBN: 0615994148
ISBN-13: 978-0615994147 (KALM)

This is a work of fiction. Names, characters, places, and incidents either are the product of the author's imagination or are used fictitiously. Any resemblance to actual persons, living or dead, events, or locales is entirely coincidental.

DEDICATION

I dedicate this book to my children: Michaela,
Sylvia, and Jonathan.

CONTENTS

ACKNOWLEDGMENTS

Thank you, Michaela, Sylvia, and Jonathan. Without you, this book would have never been a part of my reality. Thank you for your patience with me. I know that writing means a little less time I have for all of you. Above all else thank you, kids, for fully and unconditionally loving and believing in me.

Thank you, Michaela, for being the first person to read this story and give me very much appreciated and clever advice. (This would be a good place for me to also say thank you for catching many of the spelling errors I made, but that would mean admitting to the world that my nine year old can spell better than me, so I will leave that part out.)

Thank you, Amy Ellsworth, for using your editing skills and saving me from publishing a book with lot of mistakes. Thank you for working with me.

Thank you, Jason Eby, for leading me to slightly change the ending of this story. Without your advice, the girls would have had to walk away without a physical memory of Cindy. Thank you also for reading the final draft and catching the last bit of mistakes that you caught.

Thank you, Cheryl Mallow, for reading through this story backwards and forwards and then sending me advice.

1/ SCHOOL VS WEEKEND MORNINGS

The other morning I woke up with a smile on my face. I must have had an amazing dream, but I couldn't remember what it was. Do you ever wake up knowing that you just had a great dream but can't remember the details? That always drives me crazy because periodically throughout the day I feel like I am about to remember, then... nothing.

Although sometimes all the details do come back to me in an instant flash. That's always fun, isn't it, remembering something you thought you had forgotten forever? Well, I thought maybe that would happen to me the other day. Maybe I would remember my dream and then smile all over again.

As it turned out, I never did remember my dream from that night, but I did have an extraordinary day that day. It was a day full of exploring, learning, and concluded with a bit of maturing. I'm going to tell you about a magical adventure that had many faces: fear, excitement, sadness (I actually cried a few times.), and also happiness.

I woke up smiling and went to bed smiling, but in-between experienced a roller coaster of emotions!

That morning started out pretty normally. It was a Saturday morning, so we didn't have to go to school. I love not going to school! On school mornings, we have to get up and rush around while Mom yells at us the whole time to get ready even faster.

"Michaela! Sylvia! Are you girls dressed? Have you brushed your teeth? Hair? Hurry up!"

During those mornings, I usually can't find my brush. I think my sister hides it from me. When my hair isn't brushed, Mom yells even more. Sometimes while Mom is yelling, Sylvia will ask her if she has had her coffee yet. For some reason, that question brings about a much welcomed moment of silence. Mom stops yelling, gets a guilty look on her face and then laughs for a second.

My mom usually finds the brush and brushes my hair for me. Actually, it's not like she is really doing it for me, but more like she is doing it to me. While she is impatiently brushing, she adds to the torture by lecturing about how she shouldn't have to brush my hair because I should be able to take care of it myself. I always roll my eyes.

Sylvia enjoys asking Mom if her hair looks good, as I'm getting the brush ripped through mine. Sylvia knows that hers looks good, because she only asks right after she has just finished brushing. That makes me mad.

Then, as Sylvia is sitting in the doorway putting on her shoes, Mom will notice that mine are not on. So she starts yelling again.

"Michaela, you should have your shoes on by now; time is running out!"

I'm not even going to talk about what happens if I can't find my shoes.

Anyway, I have yet to see a morning where time actually ran out. We always make it out to the bus on time.

I'm sure school mornings go a lot better in your house. Your mom probably doesn't rush you all morning. And I bet your little sister doesn't hide your brush.

All of that nonsense is why I love the weekends. On the weekends, I can just lay in my bed after I wake up and watch YouTube Minecraft videos on my Kindle. (Oh! Maybe that's why I woke up with a smile!) And Sylvia lies in her bed (Unfortunately, we have to share a room.) and watches our TV. We have to wait until Mom wakes up before we are allowed to leave our room. Mom loves her sleep and Saturday and Sunday are the only days she gets to sleep in.

It's not too bad, really, because our baby brother usually wakes her up shortly after we wake. So it's not like we have to wait in our room forever and starve to death. I say that because we are not allowed to eat food in our room. That means we have to wait for mom to get up before we can eat breakfast. I can only imagine how hungry I would get if Jonathan wasn't around to be mom's weekend alarm clock.

I bet you get to leave your room when you wake up in the mornings and make yourself breakfast, don't you? You probably even get to eat in your bed, if you want. Or, even better, I bet your mom gets up before you and has your breakfast ready by the time you roll out of bed.

That sort of, just an itty-bit, makes me jealous.

2/ STOP ARGUING AND PLAY

I love my baby brother, but I'm a little jealous that he takes up so much of Mom's time. He was born a few months ago, so he still doesn't know how to play. He is actually pretty boring, if you ask me. I don't know why Mom has to spend so much time taking care of him. Playing with me would be more amusing. Oh well, at least I have my sister to horse around with, even if she does make me angry most of the time.

Yesterday morning, for example, I was eating my cereal and Sylvia sat down and started yelling that while she was in the bathroom, I took a bite of her cereal. I didn't even touch her cereal. I had my own. Besides, I don't want her gross germs. So then, after I told her I didn't take any, she hit me. She hit me and I didn't even do anything! Oh, she makes me furious!

All Mom said was, "You two stop fighting!"

That's all Mom ever says, even if I didn't do anything. When Mom wasn't looking, I hit Sylvia back, so she started crying. And then -Can you believe this?- I got in trouble!

I bet when your sister hits you, your mom sticks up for you and sends your sister to her room. You are lucky.

However if it were not for my sister, I wouldn't have anyone to play with. We live in the middle of a corn field and a lot of trees. No kids around here to hang out with, just trees and bugs. Oh, and our cat. Oh yeah, and my baby brother but he doesn't count because, like I already said, he is too little to play.

Our cat is actually missing right now, but I'm not worried yet because he wanders off for a few days at a time. He disappears about once a week. Maybe he has a secret home somewhere other than ours. I don't know what he does while he is gone, but sometimes when he comes back, he is all scratched up. One time, Sylvia wanted to put a Band-Aid on his scratches but I told her that was dumb because Band-Aids wouldn't stick to his fur.

Sylvia got mad at me and started yelling. That put Mom on the warpath because we woke her from a nap.

Mom doesn't like it when Sylvia and I are rowdy or argue while she is taking a nap or sleeping in. We have learned one thing, and that is, if we wake up Mom, we get into big trouble! Even though we know better, sometimes we forget to stay quiet, and oh boy do we get it!

That Saturday afternoon, right after lunch, Mom told us to go out to the backyard and play so the baby could take a nap, which also meant go outside and play so mom could take a nap. But that's ok because we can be as loud as we want out there. We don't get into any trouble outside as long as we stay in the backyard.

Mom doesn't let us go in the front yard because we live on a busy street. There are a lot of very fast and very big trucks that drive past our house. It is a country road, but it is one of the main highways between our city and the next. Mom says we could get smashed like a grape if we go out in the road, and that would make her cry. I don't want to make mom cry, and I don't want to die, so I stay in the backyard.

I didn't want to ride my bike, so I asked Sylvia if she would like to swing. We have a huge swing set that Dad built. Our dad builds a lot of things. One time, he let me help him build steps for our back deck. It was fun, until I smashed my finger with the hammer. After that, I didn't feel like helping him anymore. Sylvia finished helping him for me; she never smashed her finger. She is better with tools than I am, but I am not going to tell her that!

I swing better than Sylvia. I can swing really high. I am very talented! While swinging really high, I can sing the whole "Don't Mine at Night" song with my eyes closed. (That is my favorite Minecraft song. Have you heard it?) Sylvia can't get her swing to move. She just sits there and doesn't rock her body, or move her feet the right way. Well, she isn't going to get very high on the swing just sitting there.

Yup, I swing better than her, and I have no problem telling her that.

While we were walking out to the swings, I noticed my shoe was untied. I completely forgot about that though, because I started to think about my birthday party. I am going to be ten soon. My mom asked me what kind of birthday party I want to have. I told her a Minecraft party, of course! I can't wait! It is going to be epic! My mom always makes our birthday cakes. She puts a real toy on top, next to the candles. I can't wait to see what kind of Minecraft toy she finds for my cake!

As we were climbing onto our swings, I asked Sylvia what kind of birthday party she wanted. She said she wanted a surprise party. A surprise party? I asked her what kind of surprise she thought she would have if she already knew she was going to have it? She told me she didn't know, but couldn't wait to find out, and hoped it included puppies. I don't think Sylvia understands what a surprise party really is. I guess she doesn't know because she is only going to be eight. That is a whole two years less than me in learning how life works.

Sylvia loves puppies, so I'm not surprised she wants a puppy birthday party theme. We used to have a puppy named Odin. He was a big puppy. He ran away one day and never came back. That made my dad and Sylvia very sad. I was sad too, but I decided to look on the bright side and was glad we still had our cat. My mom was also a little sad, but she decided to look on the bright side and was glad she didn't have to clean up dog hair anymore.

After a few minutes, Sylvia asked me to give her a push, but my swing had already gotten really high and fast. I didn't want to get down. I felt like I was flying when I closed my eyes. I LOVE that feeling. (When my eyes are closed, I pretend I'm flying over the top of the trees.)

Then Sylvia said that she didn't want to swing anymore; she wanted to look for bugs. She didn't care that she was interrupting me. Actually, there are only a few things Sylvia does care about: puppies, bugs, and coloring. Oh, and whether or not someone took a bite of her cereal.

I didn't want to look for bugs, but I told her

I would go for a walk because I do love to explore. Sylvia wanted to walk in the woods because there are more bugs by all the trees. I thought that sounded like an excellent place to go exploring. Also, it would give me a chance to check on my favorite tree. So, I jumped out of my swing when it was all the way forward and up at the highest point. Talk about feeling like flying!

3/ SECRETS

We have a big forest in our backyard. We like to pretend that the trees are alive. Yes, I know trees really are alive, but we like to pretend that they are just like people, and each have their own personalities. (That is personification; I just learned that word in school!)We also give the trees names. My favorite tree is named Kasidy. I like to sit next to Kasidy and pretend she has a lot of stories she wants to tell me.

However, even though she wants to tell me, Kasidy does not divulge. She explains to me that will not release her stories because they are secrets. She stores them inside of her leaves. That makes me mad because I love stories, especially secret stories, and I want to hear all of hers. I bet a tree as old as Kasidy has a lot of great stories. She might be old enough to have stories about dinosaurs, or about cavemen. But she never tells them to me, even though I open up to her all the time. Not fair!

I get upset thinking about Kasidy's leaves. Storing all those secrets is extremely burdensome. So much so that, every year when it gets cooler, after the hot summers, the leaves turn a different color and then fall off. I think it is because they get weighed down by the secrets. Eventually the secrets get too heavy to hold and the leaves have to let go. It is so sad.

Do you know how it feels to keep a secret, especially if it's a bad one? Secrets can make you feel like you have extra weight inside of you. Sometimes it gets to be too much and it feels like you are going to burst. So instead of letting go, like Kasidy's leaves, you tell someone. You just can't hold it in anymore. Sometimes it's bad to give away secrets, but sometimes it's distressing not to tell secrets. It's a tricky sort of thing; knowing when you shouldn't tell and when you should.

My mom said that if someone ever hurt us and then told us to keep it a secret, that that is the kind of secret that could harm us even more by not telling. I think she meant that keeping that kind of secret inside could cause more damage, because it would allow the person to keep hurting us without anyone ever finding out.

Mom said that we should always tell her if we are ever told to keep that kind of secret, because only a bad person would hurt a kid. Mom said she could protect us from that kind of person, if we promise to tell her those kinds of secrets. It doesn't matter if the person is a kid, teenager, or adult, Mom wants us to tell.

On the other hand, if your best friend reveals that she has a crush on the boy who sits next to her during math class, you should NEVER tell that kind of secret. That is the wrong type of secret to share because then your best friend wouldn't trust you anymore. I would be heartbroken if my best friend didn't trust me anymore. Therefore if she ever tells me who she has a crush on, I promise I would never repeat it to anyone else.

While I was saying hi to my tree, Sylvia found a rollie pollie bug. She had it in her hand and was rolling it around in her palm. She gets so excited about bugs. Yuck! After I told her the bug was gross, we started walking again, heading further into the woods.

We had been walking for a little while when I noticed my shoe was still untied. I forgot about it again though, because I started to think about water. I was getting thirsty. I remember telling Sylvia that maybe we should head back home. And then right after I said that, I looked back at her. She was just standing there looking around.

I looked around to see what was distracting her and realized what she was thinking. We had never been that far into the woods. We had no idea where we were or which direction we should walk to get back home. We were lost.

I pointed toward an odd looking bent over tree and told her we should see where heading in that direction would take us. She shrugged and we started walking.

4/ GHOST HOUSE

After about two minutes, I think it was two minutes because it wasn't really very long at all, we abruptly stopped walking. We were standing in front of a big-huge-ginormous old house. The house was covered over with plants, vines, roots, tree stems, and leaves. It was creepy!

No one could have lived in the house because the windows and doors were all missing. The front steps of the house were broken and bent out of shape because a tree's roots were growing up through the middle of the steps. The tree was huge. It looked as though the roots were trying to reclaim the land that the front steps had taken. Looking at the house reminded me that we were definitely not in our backyard anymore.

Inside my head, I could hear Mom's voice saying, "Stay in the backyard!"

Then I really heard Sylvia's voice say, "Let's go inside and look!"

Oh man, we were going to get into big trouble! I knew Mom was going to be very mad if she looked out back and didn't see us playing in the yard. But I just couldn't help myself! I love to explore, and there was this big, awesome, empty, old house right in front of us.

"Well, okay," I caught myself saying, "only if we hurry though. We need to get home before Mom notices we are gone. Yeah, let's go inside and explore!"

What would you have done? Would you have run home, or gone into the house? I bet you are like me, and your curiosity would have been begging you to go inside, so you would have. Am I right?

I couldn't believe we didn't know about this place. The house was awesome! I imagined us taking it over and making a huge fort. We could make it a girls only clubhouse! I was elated by all the ideas that were popping up in my head. Sylvia and I had stumbled on the best discovery ever!

"This is so cool! Who lives here?" Sylvia asked. "Maybe it's a ghost's house! Or, Michaela, maybe it's a zombie mansion!"

Darn, I wished she hadn't said that because (I will admit to you but not Sylvia.) then I got a little scared to go in.

"No, Sylvia, ghosts and zombies are only on TV, and this is not The Walking Dead's farmhouse. This is an abandoned house. Whoever lived here left it a long time ago."

I wasn't going to tell her she had succeeded in getting me scared of whatever ghost or zombie probably wasn't living in that house.

I took a step forward and thought to myself, this is what it must feel like to be brave. I was scared, but I was going to go in and make sure my sister and I didn't get hurt while we were exploring the house.

We walked up to the front steps. They were covered with so many weeds and tree roots that it was hard to see each step. I told Sylvia to be careful and stay to the side of the steps. We successfully climbed the steps and stood just outside the front door. My heart was really pounding! The front door was gone, so we could see right into the house.

From where I was standing, I could make out a few of the things inside. It looked like a couple tables and a few chairs were in the back of the room. I could also see a bookshelf against one wall. It was dark in there, but not too dark to see because there were so many windows.

The glass from all the windows was missing or broken, and there were no curtains. That allowed a lot of sunlight into the house. Still, it was darker than a normal house. Not only was it creepy, but it was dirty and rancid. We were not inside yet, but I could smell something that was making my nose wish it had a cold, so it would be full of snot instead of that horrible smell.

"It smells like doo doo in here," Sylvia whined as she walked through the doorway.

I laughed because she said doo doo.

I don't know how she does it, but she never seems scared. I guess she will never know what it feels like to be brave, because you have to be scared of something before you can be brave of something. I know that because I'm almost ten years old. That gives me double-digit wisdom!

After I followed her into the house, my nose needed my hand to cover it. Whew! What was that smell!? We were standing in a big, dirty, front room, maybe the living room. The wall paper on the walls was falling off. It looked like a present that was slowly being unwrapped; the paper slowly being torn off. But the feel of the room wasn't as enjoyable as getting a present usually feels. The room had me feeling lonely. Maybe like a present that started to get unwrapped but never got completely opened because, for some reason, it was suddenly forgotten.

As we walked further into the room, we noticed a big staircase at the back. The staircase seemed to go up, and up, and up, forever. I couldn't see where the top landing was. It was creepy, but I couldn't help wonder what was up the stairs. Maybe we would find treasure that someone forgot to take with them!

Or maybe Sylvia's ghost was up there. Or worse, zombies could have trapped themselves in one of the upstairs rooms. Jeez, I was so glad ghosts and zombies exist only on TV! But treasure is not only on TV. Treasure can be real!

"Let's go up!" Sylvia squealed.

I was so curious by then that I also couldn't wait to get up there.

"Be careful, Sylvia! The steps might be broken. Stay close to the wall and hold the handrail," I warned as we began to climb the biggest and darkest and dirtiest set of stairs.

5/ MYSTERY

I had Sylvia go in front of me, so I could catch her if she fell back. Creek complained the next step, as she rose up onto it. Sylvia looked so small on the steps as she was climbing them. She had never before seemed fragile to me. Normally, she just looks annoying while she makes me mad by taking my toys, or pretty much everything that she does. But seeing her in that light (or lack thereof), made me feel like I needed to protect her. From what, though, I did not yet know.

We kept climbing the stairs, slowly. As I was taking another step, I noticed my shoe was still untied. Darn it! I really needed to stop and get that shoe tied. I was about to tell Sylvia to wait a minute so I could tie it, but I never got the words out of my mouth...

BOOM! BOOM! BOOM!

"Ahhhh!!!!" We yelled at the same time!

She almost fell backwards, but she was still holding the handrail, so she caught herself.

BOOM! BOOM! BOOM!

We heard the banging again. We were not climbing up the steps anymore. As a matter of fact, I wanted to run down the steps as fast as I could!

"It's coming from the door at the top of the stairs!"

"What is it?" even though I knew she didn't know, I asked.

"I don't know, Michaela, the door is shut. Maybe it's zombies trying to get out. They heard us on the steps and want a snack."

I was wondering if we should go up and open the door or if we should listen to my gut and run away, when Sylvia made up my mind for me. She started running up the stairs very fast as she said, "I'm going to open it!"

"WAIT! Sylvia, you don't know what's up there," I screamed. But I was too late.

She had reached the top of the stairs and was at the door. She had already gotten it open a crack before I got up there to stop her.

Swoosh! Out from behind the door ran our black cat, Mystery!

Mystery ran down the steps so fast that he was just a big blur, but I knew it was him. Then he must have realized it was us because he turned around and ran just as fast back up the steps. He started pawing at our legs and meowing. Mystery had been missing for a couple of days, and it seemed he was very happy he found us.

I wondered if Mystery was in that house the whole time he was missing. He must have been hungry! I was really glad to see him! I can still remember, I was three years old when he found us. He was just sitting on our porch one morning.

We didn't know where he came from or how he found our porch. Mom and Dad said we could keep him, and I could name him. I had the perfect name. It was Mystery, because it was a mystery to us where he came from, and he was a black cat; it seemed very fitting. Mom and Dad loved the name.

Sylvia and I petted him for a few minutes and then told him to go home and get some food. He went down the steps meowing all the way. I'm not sure if he was happier that he had seen us or that he was free and able to go home to eat.

"Mystery must have been pushing on this door and that is what was making that boom boom sound," Sylvia explained.

"Yeah, and he must have been pooping downstairs and that is what was making that doo doo smell," I laughed back at her.

I looked around the room we were standing in, and I realized it must have been a little girl's room at some point in time. Part of the walls still had pink paint on them. But most of the paint had peeled off and had collected on the floor next to the walls.

"A little girl used to live here. The walls are crying; I think her room misses her."

Sylvia had just verbalized what I was thinking; it did look like tears running down the wall.

As soon as we took a few steps further into the room, I felt a cold chill. I couldn't explain where the chill had come from, because it was in the middle of a very hot summer. The cold chill gave me goose bumps all over my arms, so I started rubbing them to get rid of the bumps. Suddenly, Sylvia let out a loud gasp that made me jump. The hair on the back of my neck instantly stood up.

I turned to face her and screamed, "WHAT!"

6/ THE ROCKING HORSE

"Look! Look at that rocking horse. It's so pretty!"

She was right. The rocking horse in the corner of the room was beautiful! It was the only thing in the room. It looked brand new; no dust, no dirt, and no paint falling off. The wooden horse had been painted white with blue eyes. Its mouth was open a little so you could see a pink tongue behind white teeth. The rocking horse looked as if it was laughing at us.

I was questioning how the horse could be in this dirty, old, falling down house and still look brand new when Sylvia asked, "I wonder what its name is?" Instead of waiting for an answer, she ran toward the horse.

That's when I got the worst feeling I have ever had in my entire life. It felt like I was instantly getting physically sick. And it's hard to explain, but it also felt like the room was getting smaller, like it was caving in on me. I just knew I was watching Sylvia run toward danger.

"STOP!" I tried to warn, but it was too late.

Sylvia jumped on the rocking horse and started rocking back and forth. "WEE! WEE! WEE!" she was laughing.

I couldn't help myself; I let out a smile because she was having fun. For a second, I forgot about the sick feeling and the fact that the rocking horse did not look like it belonged in that house. I started to take a step toward her and the horse when I was stopped dead in my tracks by a very loud and very angry little girl's voice.

"HEY! GET OFF MY ROCKING HORSE!"

It scared me so much that I jumped back about three feet. Sylvia and I looked at each other with wide eyes. We both opened our mouths to scream, but I only heard my own because Sylvia instantly vanished.

Poof!

Gone!

No more rocking, no more laughing, no more Sylvia. All that was left was the rocking horse in the corner of the room, laughing, and me in the middle of the room, screaming.

"SYLVIA! SYLVia! SYlvia! sylvia…" After a few moments, I found myself whispering her name. I guess my voice got tired. Or maybe, it was too scared to continue screaming.

"Where are you?" I whispered. There was no answer from Sylvia, but the rocking horse was standing there smirking at me. I was terrified; I didn't know what to do. I just stood there shaking and staring at the horse.

When I was able to move again, I backed up against the wall that was farthest away from the rocking horse. Then, I slid down to the floor. How could she have disappeared? Mommy and Daddy said that kind of stuff, you know, the scary stuff from movies, isn't real. Well, if it isn't real, then where was my little sister? And, who in the heck's voice was that?

Should I have run home to tell Mommy? What would I have told her? She wouldn't have believed me anyway. Maybe the police would come and arrest me because they would all think I made my sister disappear. I didn't know what I was going to do. I only knew that I had to get Sylvia back.

That's when I realized something; I must really and truly love my sister. As I sat there in that creepy room, I couldn't imagine my life without her. She was my best friend, and I never knew it until then. I was usually too busy thinking about how annoying she was and how mad she could make me. I realized I should have spent more time thinking about all the positive qualities she has instead of the negative.

She knows how to make the people around her laugh and have a good time. When Sylvia tells a story, she expresses it with her eyes just as much as her words. Her eyes are so animated that often I get lost in her world just by watching her eyes talk. A lot of times, most of the time actually, we really do have fun together when we play.

Sitting alone in that room, I had an epiphany. I thought that I may have been too mean to Sylvia. What if the reason she always irritated me so much was because she was reacting negatively to the way I treated her? Maybe, if I wasn't so mean to her, she would not have been so annoying and, at times, mean back to me.

For example, Sylvia likes to feel important, and there have been times that I would go out of my way to try and make her feel insignificant. I wish I hadn't done that. Sylvia actually is quite remarkable! What if I never got to see her again? What if she never got to hear me tell her that I love her and that she really is awesome and my best friend?

Then it came to me, a great idea, but a frightening one. I had to get on the rocking horse. I had to get on and start rocking and then maybe, just maybe, I would end up where Sylvia went. I could save her! My heart was rapidly beating; I thought it might jump out of my chest and run home to Mommy. But there was no time for that.

It was time to be brave.

I told my heart to calm down as I stood up and tried to move forward. That, I then knew for certain, was definitely what being brave feels like. I just wanted to run out of that bedroom and out of that house, but I wouldn't do that. I had to get on the rocking horse. I begged my legs to get up and walk forward. The rocking horse still seemed to be laughing at me.

They did it; my legs moved, and then I was able to climb on the rocking horse. It actually wasn't so bad. At first, I rocked slowly and then I started rocking faster and faster. After a few glides, I almost forgot that I was scared, because rocking was fun, almost as enjoyable as swinging. I let a smile escape my lips.

"HEY! GET OFF MY ROCKING HORSE!"

Poof!

7/ THE BLACKNESS

What the heck? The next thing I knew, I was sitting in the darkest place I had ever been in my life. It wasn't like a dark room at night, because in dark rooms at night, I can still see some things. No, I was not sitting in *just* dark. I was in blackness. I couldn't see my own hand when I put it right in front of my face. I couldn't see anything, except black!

Stop reading this for a second and close your eyes, and then put your hand tightly over them. That is where I was; inside of that blackness!

I noticed I was holding my breath at the same moment I realized I could hear Sylvia crying.

"Sylvia! Oh my gosh, Sylvia, is that you!?" I had to ask because I could only hear her. I couldn't see her.

"Michaela?" Sylvia whispered in-between cries.

Even though I was more terrified than I had ever been in my life, I was grateful that I got on the rocking horse. What if I never braved it and left Sylvia in the blackness, alone, crying, forever? Actually, I didn't want to think about her being in there all alone. So, I told her to talk to me. I wanted her voice to tell my ears to tell my legs where to go, so I could hug her.

While Sylvia told me how frightened she was, my ears directed my legs toward her. Then I bumped right into her. I sat down and grabbed her and we hugged and cried, together, in the blackness. We hugged like that for a long time. I was afraid to let go and lose her again.

"Sissy, I love you. Thank you for finding me! I thought I was disappeared alone forever."

"Where are we Sylvia?" I had to ask, even though I knew she was clueless.

She told me she didn't know and that she had been too scared to move since she had been there. I figured we needed to see if there was a way out instead of sitting there any longer. I asked her to hold my hand, and explained that we should stand up and walk forward, very slowly, until we reached a wall. After we found a wall, maybe we could find a door.

Sylvia grabbed my hand and we took itty bitty steps forward. It was a peculiar sensation, walking forward while my eyes couldn't see. Not only was it strange, but it was extremely stressful. I was waiting for my feet to trip on something or to fall into a hole. At the same time, I was petrified my hand was going to touch something slimy or furry.

I was trying not to let my brain think of all the horrible stuff that could happen or the creepy things I could bump into when, thump, my foot hit something solid. I held my breath and cautiously raised my hand and felt a smooth, flat, and big surface. Yup, just like a wall should have felt. Thank goodness!

I told Sylvia we needed to follow the wall around the room until we found a door. I explained we would count each turn we came to because a room should have four corners in it. When we have counted to five that would mean we had probably gone around the whole room and then some. We gradually walked sideways, and did not let go of hands. I wasn't going to let Sylvia's hand go for anything, not even for a flash light!

As we were side stepping, Sylvia told me she never wanted to ride another rocking horse again. That made me giggle, despite the fact that I was on edge; it just seemed funny in that moment. Then, I couldn't stop my giggles from turning into laughter. In the middle of that nonsensical situation, I was suddenly afflicted with a laughing fit. Then Sylvia caught the fit and joined me.

We were both laughing hysterically; we couldn't stop ourselves until, bump; we hit the first corner in the room. Bumping into the corner made us knock into each other and that caused our heads to bang together. That wasn't very funny so we stopped laughing.

Slowly, we continued to creep around the room until we counted five corners. There was no door. There was nothing but walls, corners, a floor, and the blackness. My emotions were all over the place. I had never felt like that before. I couldn't give it a name, even if you had asked me. We were trapped in blackness and I definitely was more than just scared!

"I want Mommy!"

"Me too!" We hardly ever agree except when it comes to ice cream and exploring. Too bad we didn't decide to get ice cream that afternoon instead of going exploring.

I told her we should sit down and think but not let go of hands. As we sat, she asked me to tell her a story. We always like to hear stories. Sometimes at night, instead of having Mom read to us, we ask her to make up a story to tell us. She has made up some amazing stories. I found myself wishing I was listening to one of Mom's tales, instead of having to recite one.

"Tell me the story about the library. I like that story; I think it is going to be scary and then it turns out to be funny."

Actually I was glad she asked me to tell her a story, because it was so black in the room we were in that I was actually starting to hear the darkness, even though I couldn't see it. That might not make any sense, but that is exactly just how dark it was.

It seemed the blackness was whispering scary stories. I didn't want to let my ears hear anything that was coming from the darkness that surrounded us. It was trying to tell me stories about all the spooky stuff I have ever seen or thought. I didn't want to be frightened anymore. I didn't want to think about zombies or ghosts. Also, I didn't want to think about being stuck in that dark room forever, so I started talking. I told Sylvia the story about the library...

8/ IT

"One day, a little girl went to the library with her mom. When they walked into the library, her mom told her to stay in the children's books area. The little girl promised her mom she would be good. The mom walked away, to find a book for herself. The little girl started looking through the children's books.

"The librarian, a nosey type of woman, noticed the little girl was by herself and walked over to her. She asked the little girl if she needed any help finding a book. The little girl said, 'I love monsters! Do you have any books about monsters?' The librarian told her that she had a few books about monsters but they were upstairs and unfortunately, no one could go upstairs that day."

"What was the little girl's name?" Sylvia has to interrupt and ask me a question every time I tell a story.

I mean was it really important what the little girl's name was. Couldn't I just call her little girl for the whole story? Did I really need to give her a name when I'm only going to be talking about her for a few more minutes? Jeesh!

"Trista, Trista is her name. Happy now?"

Sylvia told me she was happy, gave my hand a little squeeze, and asked me to finish the story.

"Trista asked if the librarian would mind going up to get the monster books, but the librarian told her again, that no one was allowed upstairs for a few days. The librarian mentioned there were things upstairs that were not to be messed with. She explained that until they get the upstairs of the library reorganized NO ONE was allowed up there. It was just too dangerous. As the librarian looked down her nose at Trista, she asked if Trista understood.

"Trista promised the librarian that she understood and would not go upstairs. Trista was sad, but decided she would just look at all the books on the shelves where she was until her mom came back.

"Trista was walking through the aisles and looking at books when she noticed a door that had a sign that read, stairs. She looked around to see if anyone was watching her. No one was looking. The librarian was busy helping an older lady check out some books. And, her mom was nowhere to be seen. So, without giving it much thought, Trista ran to the door and opened it.

"She walked through the door and shut it quickly but quietly so that no one would notice her, or hear the door trying to tell on her by making loud sounds as it closed. There were no lights on and she couldn't find the light switch. The switch was probably on the other side of the door. It was dark, but not too dark to see because there was a window at the top of the stairs that allowed some light into the stairwell.

"Trista slowly climbed the stairs. She didn't know why but the hair on the back of her neck was standing up and goose bumps grew up her arms. For some reason, she was getting scared. Maybe because it was a little too dark and she couldn't quite see what was in the room at the top of the stairs.

"Or maybe it was because she knew she was doing something she was told not to do and would get into big trouble if she was found in the stairwell. Either way, it didn't matter, she was already there and one by one she crept up the steps until she finally reached the top.

"She looked around the room.

"The light from the window lit the room enough that she could see that it was full of shadows, dark boxes, shelves, and tables. Even with the window light, it was still too dark to make out the details of everything she was looking at. Trista saw a row of bookshelves on the opposite side of the room and decided that was probably where the monster books were. It was while she was walking over to the bookshelf that she thought the reason why the librarian told her no one was allowed to go upstairs was probably because it was such a mess!

"Boxes and tables and chairs were everywhere. She saw a few ladders and some paint cans. She guessed they were in the middle of redecorating. She quietly continued to walk over toward the bookshelves. When she reached the first shelf, she instantly saw a row of books about monsters. Trista was thrilled and started pulling the books off the bookshelf. Because she was so distracted by the books that she was finding, it took her a couple minutes to hear the heavy breathing that was coming from behind her."

"Michaela! Can you imagine if we started to hear some heavy breathing in here! I don't know what I would do. Now, I'm getting even more scared, maybe you should not finish this story. Maybe you should tell me a different story about a bright sunny day and happy puppies that are running around a pool. Then maybe one of the puppies knocks over a table that had a whole bunch of cheeseburgers on it and so all the other puppies run over and start eating. Yeah, that sounds like a really good story Michaela! I don't want to hear any more about heavy breathing!"

"Sylvia, will you stop it and let me finish the story! I'm not going to change it now and start talking about puppies. I am already halfway done. Besides, you know it is sort of funny at the end. So stop being a scaredy-cat, and stop interrupting me; just listen!"

Unfortunately realizing how much I love my sister, didn't mean that I would never again get annoyed with her.

After I took a few deep breaths, I continued with the story.

"It was while Trista was looking through a book about a one-eyed-purple-people-eater that she realized she could hear heavy and steady breathing. She stopped looking at the book and turned around slowly. She didn't see anything behind her except a huge box with a big blanket over the top of it. She couldn't tell what was under the blanket, but she knew for certain that it was where the breathing was coming from. She couldn't help herself, even as scared as she had become, she slowly took a few small steps towards the blanket.

"Trista forced herself to keep taking a few more steps, and with each step the breathing got a little louder. It sounded as if a giant man was sleeping under the blanket. She came to a corner of the blanket. It was much larger than the box it was covering, which she could only guess was some type of cage. The blanket was so big that it draped across the floor a few feet around each side of the box, or cage, or whatever it was.

"Trista mustered up some courage and reached down, then slowly pulled on the blanket. At first, nothing happened. However, after she had been pulling a few seconds, the blanket started falling off the cage, toward her. She kept pulling until the blanket completely fell to the floor.

"She was looking at a very big cage. It was about the size of one of the bathrooms in Trista's house, but not as high. It was only about as tall as her daddy. At first, she didn't see anything inside the cage, but she could still hear the steady breathing. She took a few steps closer and as she did she tripped over the blanket and fell, with a thud, to the floor.

"The heavy breathing stopped. Trista's heart began to race and she held her breath as she slowly got up onto her knees and forced herself to look up. On the side of the cage, next to a very small door, she saw a sign that read, DO NOT STARE IT IN THE EYES!

"Do not stare it in the eyes? She wondered what that meant exactly. Trista looked around the inside of the cage. She was looking for whatever *it* was that the sign was warning about. She figured that it must also be the same thing that was making the heavy breathing before she fell.

"Then she saw it.

"It was a little bluish-grey furry thing lying on the floor of the cage. It was watching her. As soon as she noticed, she quickly looked away from its eyes. Trying to figure out what it was, Trista moved her eyes to look over its body. She had never in her entire life seen anything like it. It was about the size of a puppy and it was furry like a puppy, but it definitely was not a puppy!

"It had two legs, not four. It had no knees, but it did have feet at the end of its legs. The feet were webbed, like a frog's feet. Its body was square and furry and it only had one arm. The arm was not furry and it had no solid shape. It was just blubbery and floppy and there was no hand or fingers at the end of the arm.

"Its head was the weirdest part of all. It was shaped like a heart. The mouth was a circle at the bottom of the heart and there was no nose. Its eyes were at the top of the heart, one in the middle of each of the curves. Its eyes were glowing green. There were no black pupils.

"The green glowing eyes were staring at Trista, and she was staring at them.

"Oh no! The sign!

"DO NOT STARE IT IN THE EYES!

"It was too late, Trista tried to look away once she realized she was staring at it, but it started making a loud roar and she just couldn't look away. The first few roars sounded like a lion's roar. After about the fifth roar, it sounded more like a loud jet! The roaring was getting louder, and louder, and the monster started getting bigger, and bigger!

"Trista wanted to run but she still couldn't bring herself to look away. The monster continued to stare at her while it was roaring as loud as a jet and growing as big as the cage! Pretty soon the monster was going to be so big that the cage would break into pieces! Trista's heart was racing so fast she thought for a second it was going to burst at the same time as the cage.

"She heard the cage crack. One of the bars broke in half. Then another bar flew across the room. Another of the bars broke loose and fell to the floor. At this rate, the monster would be free from the cage at any second. Even still, Trista was so scared that she couldn't move.

"Then, the monster yelled, 'I'm going to get you!'

"That did it! Trista turned around and ran! She ran through the room and down the stairs. She didn't look at anybody in the library; she just ran right through the aisles and then out the front door. It wasn't until she was outside running down the sidewalk that she looked behind her for the first time.

"The monster was just getting out of the library's front door. It was still chasing her and it was running very fast! Trista continued running down the sidewalk and then across the street.

"ROAR! She could hear the monster behind her.

"ROAR! It sounded louder!

"ROAR! It was almost on top of her!

"ROAR!

"Oh no! She tripped and fell down!

"Trista covered her head just as the monster jumped on top of her. She felt the monster's gross flabby arm touch the top of her head. She thought its gross arm was going to tear her apart so that its weird mouth could eat her up.

"Trista thought about her mom and how sad her mom would be to learn that her daughter was eaten up by a monster. All this was happening because Trista made a mistake and didn't keep her promises to her mom and the librarian. She thought, why, oh why, didn't she just stay downstairs and be a good girl. She also thought she would never get to eat another ice cream cone again.

"Trista thought how she would never see any of her friends again. She thought she would never get to read another book or watch another Pokémon show. She thought she was never going to get to pick out a beautiful wedding dress, or go to a really cool place for her honey moon. Trista was just about to scream out in frustration for all the things in life that she was going to miss out on because she made one mistake, when she heard, 'Tag! You're it!'

"And then, she felt the monster jump off her and could hear it running down the sidewalk, away from her.

"'What! WHAT!?! Tag I'm it!?!' Trista sat up and watched it run away. She couldn't believe her ears or her eyes. Was it really just playing tag with her instead of trying to eat her? She started to laugh and then she couldn't stop laughing. She had feared for her life, but it was just playing a game!

"She lay on the sidewalk and continued to laugh so hard that she almost peed her pants. Trista was incredibly happy that she wasn't going to miss out on her life after all.

She was so grateful that she made a vow to do her best to never misbehave again.

"That time she ended up getting really lucky and the monster was a nice one who just wanted to play games; teach her a lesson. But next time the story could end up differently; she might not get so lucky again. She continued to laugh and laugh until her mom ran out of the library and down the sidewalk to her."

9/ A CURIOUS GIRL

"I do love that story!" Sylvia exclaimed.

I wished I could have seen the smile that I could hear on her face.

I agreed with her. Telling the story gave me a nice break from being scared.

"What are we going to do now?"

"Let's slide along the floor and see if we can find a trap door or hole of some kind," I said more hopefully than I actually felt.

"Ok. I really want out of this darkness! Please don't let go of my hand!" Sylvia begged.

It was difficult sliding along the floor and feeling around with one hand for anything that might be a way out while our other hands were holding each other. But we never let go.

My heart was pounding. My brain kept thinking what if we touched something gross? What if there was a hole and we fell through it and got hurt? The worst thoughts of all were the ones that questioned what if there was someone, or something, else in the room with us. Oh my gosh, it was horrifying; I couldn't find a way to get my brain to stop terrorizing me with the dark thoughts.

The darkness must also have been taunting Sylvia because she cried, "Michaela, wait! I can't move."

I asked her why not and told her if we were going to find a way out we had to keep moving and feeling around the room. She started crying and said she was scared. Normally, I would have gotten really annoyed at Sylvia for crying and not doing what I wanted her to do. However, I could sympathize that time because I was also petrified, and since I'm almost ten and she is only almost eight, she must have been a lot more scared than me.

Instead of getting mad and calling her a scaredy-cat, I gave her a big hug. She firmly held me until she stopped crying. We let go of each other but kept a tight grasp of hands.

I encouraged, "Sylvia, we have to keep moving. We have to find a way to get out of this despicable darkness. I won't let go of your hand. I won't lose you again. We can do this together!"

Right when I said the word together, a little girl appeared in front of us! I don't know how I could see her because it was too dark to see anything. I still couldn't see myself, or Sylvia, or anything for that matter, except the little girl standing in front of us.

Sylvia gasped, "Oh! Look, a girl!"

I was happy to know I wasn't the only one who could see her. It was curious seeing a girl surrounded by the blackness. Thank God she was friendly looking and not scary looking. I don't think I could have handled it if she looked ghoulish! After studying us for a few moments, she smiled and said hello.

We both whispered, hi.

"Well, I told you two to get off my rocking horse. You would have never gotten stuck here if you would have stayed off my horse."

Sylvia and I slid closer together and I put my arm around her. The little girl must have known she frightened us because she said, "Don't be scared. I don't want to hurt you. I just want to play. My name is Cindy, and I haven't had anyone to play with in a very long time.

"This used to be my house. That was my room you were in and that was my very favorite toy, my rocking horse. It is the only thing I have left of that life, and I didn't want to share it with anyone. When you got on my horse, I got mad and yelled. Then you fell into the blackness.

"Even though I was mad at first, I'm not mad anymore. I've been watching you both and I want to be friends. You guys are entertaining. I laughed when you were laughing and then bumped heads. I enjoyed your story about the library. And I like how close you two are, and how much you love each other. It's great that you figured out you can work together to get out of this scary room.

"Now that I know I like you guys, I want to play! I don't know exactly how long it has been since I have played! I have all sorts of fun games in mind. First, we can play tea party. Then we can color. We can also play dolls and maybe some tag or basketball. Your library story made me want to play tag! It would be so much fun to run!"

Well, I didn't want to play any of that. Especially with someone (or something) that had to do with us being in that darkness. I just wanted to go home. However, after listening to her talk and thinking about it for a second, it seemed to me that somehow Cindy was going to be our way home. I just didn't understand how.

I decided to ask her. "Cindy, my sister and I are scared. Can we please just go home, now? Our mom might be very worried."

"NO!" She actually screamed at me. "You went on my rocking horse. That means you wanted to play, so we are going to play!"

She sounded mad, but I could sense that she was concerned. What she was so worried about, I did not know.

Sylvia started crying, again. It appeared Sylvia did not like Cindy, which was ok with me because I didn't like her either. She was being bossy and didn't seem to care that we just wanted to go home.

Then it occurred to me, "Cindy, if we play with you for a little bit, can we go home after that?"

She seemed hesitant but told us she would send us home after we were done playing. However, she made it clear that we had to play what she wanted to play because this was her time with us. Cindy wanted to play dolls. That didn't sound very fun to me, especially since we were still surrounded by blackness.

10/ DOLLS

"I will be the puppy doll. Michaela, you be the mommy doll. And, Sylvia, you be the baby doll."

As soon as she finished telling us our roles, I felt a doll in my hand. Unfortunately, I could not see the doll. It was still completely black where we were. I assumed Sylvia had a doll in her hand too because she started to throw a fit. I should have known it was coming when Cindy said she had a toy dog but Sylvia had to be a baby.

-Remember, I told you Sylvia LOVES puppies.-

"I don't want the baby doll! I want to be the puppy."

"You will be the baby or I won't let you go home!" Cindy warned.

That made Sylvia angry; she started crying again. I told Sylvia we should play Cindy's way so, afterwards, we could get out of there.

"But, I don't want to play with her! She is mean and wants everything her way! If we are going to play, I want to be the doggie. We should all get to decide together how we are going to play," Sylvia insisted.

I thought that was a great idea, and it does make the game more fun for everyone when all the people playing get to decide together how to play. But for some reason, I didn't think Cindy was going to let us have a say in her game.

"No! I want the doggie doll. I want you to play the baby doll," Cindy sounded like she was on the verge of crying. "Now, lay down your baby doll, her diaper is dirty and she needs to be changed. Mommy doll," she looked over at me to say, "you need to change the baby's diaper and then give her a bottle."

I was wondering how I was supposed to change Sylvia's doll's diaper when I still couldn't see Sylvia, let alone her doll. It seemed apparent that Cindy could see Sylvia and me, but I guess she had forgotten that we still couldn't see each other or ourselves because of the blackness.

Sylvia interrupted my thoughts with more protests. It didn't seem like she was going to give up easily. As far as I was concerned, we were wasting time arguing.

"Cindy is the only one that knows how to get out of here. There are a lot of times when we are playing together, Sylvia, that you are bossy and have to have your way even though I don't want to play it that way.

"See how Cindy is making you feel, Sylvia? It's not nice to be bossy and always have to have your way. It makes other people not want to play with you; just like you don't want to play with Cindy. If this is how you feel when someone is treating you that way, think about how you make the other kids feel when you treat them that way."

I had an idea. "Sylvia, how about we just play the game her way, this time. Then from now on, when we play together or with anyone else, we take turns. You can have it your way on one day. Then I can have it my way on the next day. Or maybe, we could agree and make up a game that we play where we could both have our way."

Sylvia must have liked that idea because she told me ok, but the day for having it her way was going to be the first day! Ugh! I wasn't going to argue or plead with her anymore, so I just agreed.

Just then, right when we finally agreed, the blackness completely went away. I could see Sylvia! I could see myself! I could see everything! We were in an old room with a wood floor and dingy yellow wallpaper on the walls. I was so happy to be able to see again that I gave Sylvia a big hug! I noticed she had dirt all over her face and hair; it made me laugh. Sylvia was smiling at me too. I could see the tear stains running down through the dirt on her cheek.

Cindy told us we were boring her with all our talking, crying, and hugging. She didn't want to play dolls anymore. She wanted to play basketball instead. As soon as she said that, a basketball hoop appeared with three balls next to it.

Oh no! I had a sinking feeling in my tummy. Did we really have to play basketball? For a second I thought that being back in the blackness again would be more enjoyable than basketball.

11/ HORSE

I can barely throw a ball in the right direction, let alone dribble or shoot a ball. But still, I wanted to go home and I knew that meant I had to try and play basketball. So, as Mom likes to say… sometimes we just have to do things that we really don't want to do.

Luckily for Sylvia, she is good at sports and would have no problem with the game. We each picked up a ball and stood in the middle of the floor, a few feet away from the hoop.

"We are not actually going to play a game of basketball. We are going to play a game called HORSE," Cindy explained.

Oh, I love horses! But somehow I doubted that the game of Cindy's had anything to do with actual horses. She walked over next to the basketball hoop and explained how to play.

"We each stand the same distance from the hoop. We start, here, this close to the hoop. We take turns throwing our basketballs into the basket. When we get the ball in, we take a step back. If we don't get the ball in, we stay in the same spot and say the first letter of the word HORSE, H. The first person who misses enough baskets that they have spelled the word HORSE is out."

Sylvia and I took a few steps closer to the hoop so that we were standing next to Cindy. Then, Cindy threw her ball. It swooshed right through the net. Sylvia threw her ball next and it bounced off the rim onto the backboard then fell right through the net. They both took a step back and looked at me to let me know they were waiting for me to throw my ball.

I didn't want to throw the ball. I was going to end up looking stupid in front of the two of them because I can't throw.

"I don't want to play this game. I don't like basketball!"

Actually, I do like it. It looks fun. I just can't throw a ball and I'm embarrassed to try it, especially in front of people. I didn't want them to laugh at me. I knew I wouldn't make it in the hoop so why should I have even tried.

"You are going to throw your ball, or you are not going to go home," Cindy clearly stated.

In that moment, I really did not like that Cindy girl, or ghost, or whatever she was.

"Michaela, if you don't try we are going to be stuck here. I want to go home. I'm hungry; I want dinner. I will even ask Mom to make your favorite, spaghetti, even though I don't like it. Throw the ball. You were just yelling at me for not wanting to play, and now you are not playing. Do it! Remember what Mom always says, 'Just believe in yourself.'

"It's okay if you don't make it in. You don't have to be embarrassed. This really isn't about you anyway. It's about all of us playing a game, and then you and I going home!"

I still didn't want to try, but I felt even more embarrassed by the type of attention I was getting from not trying. They were annoyed. Mom does always say believe in yourself and try everything. And Sylvia was right, it wasn't about me, it was about all of us.

So, I closed my eyes and I pictured myself throwing the ball and making it in the basket. "Believe in yourself and just give it a try." I could hear Mom's voice, faintly, in my head. "It's not about winning or losing. It's about having fun while you are doing it. How will you ever have fun if you don't ever try?"

Then I looked at the ball and imagined it was filled with all my doubts instead of air. I looked up at the hoop and pretended it was a big mouth that wanted to eat all the doubts so that I wouldn't have to hold on to them anymore.

I looked up at the hoop and then at the ball again, and before I had time for more negative thoughts, I threw the ball. I was throwing away all my doubts and hoping the big mouth would swallow them up!

The ball went right through the hoop! I did it! I couldn't believe I did it! I was jumping up and down screaming when I heard Sylvia and Cindy clapping for me. I felt awesome!

Cindy said, "Now we do it again from over here where Sylvia and I are standing." Then she threw her ball and made it. Sylvia threw next and also made it in the basket.

Sylvia made it look so easy! I closed my eyes and told myself to believe and then threw the ball. It bounced off the back board and flew right back at me. Oh no! I missed! I almost starting crying, but Sylvia interrupted my pity-party.

"Michaela, you did it! You just said you couldn't even throw the ball, but you made one basket and hit the backboard this time. You do know how to throw the ball!"

She was so excited for me that I couldn't feel upset anymore.

She was right. I may not have made the basket the second time but I did throw the ball pretty far! At least I knew then that I could throw basketballs! All I had to do was believe in myself and give it a try. Now, if I want to be able to make baskets all the time, I am going to have to practice a lot, but that's ok. I learned that it's actually fun throwing the ball!

I said the letter H because I missed the basket. I was the only one with a letter. I was thinking I would get through all the letters, H. O. R. S. E, before Sylvia or Cindy missed a basket when Cindy said, "Sylvia, if you make this next shot, I'll send you two home now instead of waiting until we finish a whole game."

Sylvia's face turned into a huge smile and she said, "No problem! I can make this shot with my eyes closed!" She quickly threw the ball and it went completely over the entire hoop. Her extreme confidence overshot the ball!

Sylvia cried, "Stupid ball. It should have gone into the hoop!"

"Maybe you should have given it a little more concentration instead of bragging and being so sure of yourself. You hardly even paid attention to what you were doing. You were so sure it was just going to happen. Nothing just happens, no matter how sure of yourself you are. You always have to give everything your attention and try hard. Even if it is something you are already really good at doing," Cindy tried to explain.

"I still want to go home now!"

"Don't you like it here? Just about anything you could want is here."

"Not my baby brother, or my mom and dad. They are not here and I miss them."

"I miss my family too," Cindy sighed.

I asked her where her family was, and then, before she could answer, I asked where we were, exactly.

"Well, that is a long story and it's not a happy story," Cindy warned.

"We want to hear it anyway!"

12/ MONSTERS

"Well, ok, it just so happens that I do need to tell you my story. But don't say I didn't warn you; it's a very sad story. But first, let me tell you where I think we are. We are in an in-between world, in between the living and the dead. I have been here ever since my death."

"You are a ghost! I thought you were a ghost! I never met a ghost before, and Dad said they are not real. So even though I thought you were a ghost, I didn't want to say anything." Sylvia was so excited. "I was right, Michaela, that is a ghost's house we found!"

"Yes, I'm a ghost to you, I guess, but to me, I am just me. And I miss my family very much, but I have a job to do before I can be with them. I will explain that in a minute. My family is beyond the in-between world. They are waiting for me to do my job here so I can meet them. I haven't actually known what my job would be until you two got here, but now I know. My job is to help you!"

"Help us, how?" I asked.

"I will explain in a little bit. First, I want to tell you how I got here. That means I have to tell you how I passed away."

"Wait a minute!" I interrupted. "If you are dead and in an in-between world, why are Sylvia and I here? We aren't dead! Are we?" I couldn't believe I just asked if I was dead or not, but it really didn't make any sense. How could I be dead; I didn't die. But how could I be in the same world as, and talking to, a ghost. I was getting myself all worked up before Cindy had the chance to answer me.

"Relax, Michaela, you are alive. Both of you are unconscious right now. You see, my rocking horse was too close to the wall, and Sylvia started rocking too fast. Right after you heard me tell her to get off my rocking horse, she hit her head on the wall. She became unconscious and fell into the darkness.

"Michaela, when you heard my voice telling Sylvia to get off my rocking horse, it scared you so much that you jumped backwards and tripped on your shoelace that wasn't tied. Your shoelace made you stumble a few feet, and you fell back and hit your head on the wall. That is how you became unconscious. You really should always make sure your shoe laces are tied!"

"Wait, I got on the rocking horse after Sylvia," I protested.

"Yes, you did, sort of, that was after you became unconscious, it was a dream that you were separated from Sylvia. You were actually in the dark room, unconscious, with her. You just thought you were apart. For some reason, Michaela, you needed to learn that it's your job as a big sister to be brave and look out for your little sister and baby brother. You needed to figure that out before the darkness let you find her.

"Now, I'll tell you what happened to me.

"One afternoon, I was outside riding my bike up and down the road and a man pulled his car up next to me. I didn't know the man's name, but he knew mine. He told me that my mom had just asked him to come get me because my dad was in an accident. My mom had to leave right away for the hospital to be with my dad. The man told me that my mom asked him to take me to the hospital, so I could also be with them."

I had a feeling I might need to sit down for this story. I set my ball on the floor and then sat on top of it. I was careful to do it quietly as to not interrupt Cindy. However, once Sylvia saw me sit on my basketball, she also wanted to sit on hers.

Sylvia excused herself and then walked over to where her ball landed earlier. She dribbled the ball back to where Cindy was standing and I was sitting. Cindy had stopped the story because Sylvia had not been as quiet about getting and sitting on her ball. Once Sylvia was quiet and comfortable, Cindy continued with her story.

"My mom always told me not to talk to strangers, but I didn't really think this guy was a stranger because I often saw him drive down my street. I thought he was a neighbor. Every time he drove by me while I was riding my bike or walking, he would wave and I would wave back, you know, just to be nice. I had never talked to him before, but I had seen him so many times that he was familiar to me. Plus, he knew my name!

"After he said he had just talked to my mom and that my dad was in an accident, I wasn't really thinking about him being a stranger. I was just thinking about my dad, and I was worried and wondering if he was hurt really bad. The man told me to get in his car, and he would drive me to the hospital. He told me in order to save time, I should leave my bike right there on the side of the road, and my mom and I could get it later after we made sure my dad was alright.

"I was so concerned about my dad that I did what the man told me to do. I put my bike down in the ditch and got into his car. That was the biggest mistake of my life. It was also the last mistake of my life. That man was evil; he stole my life from me.

"You see, my dad wasn't really in a car accident. That man had never talked to my mom. The only reason he knew my name is because he saw my mom and me in a store one time, and he heard her call out my name. Then he followed us home so he knew where I lived.

"After he tricked me to get into his car, he took me to a house I had never been to before and locked me in a room. He never gave me any food or water. There was nothing I could do but cry and wish it would end. After a few days, he had hurt me so much, and I was so hungry, that physically I could not take it anymore, so I died."

"Ohh noooo!" Sylvia and I were horrified! My eyes were stinging from the pressure that the sadness tears had built up. They needed to push their way out of my eyes.

"You see," Cindy continued, "I got into a car with a stranger. I'm sure your parents have told you girls never to do that. My parents also told me, all the time, to never talk to strangers and never ever get into a stranger's car. But that man, even though he was wicked, he was smart and able to trick me.

"He looked like a nice man and dressed like a nice man and had a nice car and smiled like a nice man. But he tricked me because he was not a nice man, and I never got to see my family again.

"That all happened a very long time ago and my family has since then passed away themselves. Nothing bad happened to them, just normal deaths from living a long life. I could have had a long life too, if that man hadn't tricked me."

As Cindy was telling us this, I realized I was crying. Sylvia was also crying. I was heartbroken over what Cindy went through. I also felt guilty that a few minutes earlier, I was really mad at her and didn't like her very much. If only I had known what happened to her before we started playing, I would have been more agreeable. I bet Sylvia would have been, too. She probably would have even played the baby doll without arguing.

Oh my gosh, Cindy was just a little girl! She just made a mistake and because of it, she was taken away from her family. Through my tears, I looked over at Sylvia, and I couldn't help myself; I put my arm around her.

"Well, it is no use crying about it. Crying won't change anything; I know that; trust me. However, the good news is, that now, I can get out of this place and on to the place where my family is waiting for me. As soon as you girls got into the dark room, I knew it was you I had to help. I just didn't know, at first, how I was supposed to help. That's why I wanted to play games with you for a while. I needed to stall until I understood what it was you needed help with.

"While you guys were in the blackness, and then again while we were all playing, I noticed that you two are really great at encouraging each other. You probably fight all the time and may be very different from each other, but that is normal because you are sisters. Yet, I could tell that you love each other and would always look out for each other.

"I was watching you both and thinking how nice it must be to have a sister to share life with and look out for. That's when I realized that you two look out for each other, but what if something were to happen while you were together?

"I knew then that my job is to look out for the both of you! I had to tell you my story, and warn you about leaving your parents in crowded places or talking to strangers. Through my story, you have been reminded that not all people are nice. There actually are some real monsters that exist. Not all grown-ups do the right thing.

"Even if you think you know a person, like I thought I sort of knew that man who took me, you never really completely know if they are honest and good. And sometimes, it's not only adults who are bad. There are also stories out there of younger people, teenagers and older kids, who have hurt and killed other kids.

"Not too long ago, two teenagers tricked a boy by pretending they were his friends. He was out riding his bike one morning. They told him to go into their house and they would give him a video game that they did not want anymore. He loved video games and was curious about what they wanted to give him, and so he decided to trust the teenagers. He went into their house without asking his mom first. After the boy entered their house, they hurt him and he died.

"He thought he was going into a couple of nice teenagers' house to get something cool from them, but they tricked him. He lost his life because he trusted someone he should not have and went into a house without asking his parents. His mother and the rest of his family will never get to see him again because the sweet little boy thought all teenagers were safe to trust.

"I'm sorry to scare you girls with these stories. Mostly, I'm sorry this is the way the world can be sometimes. But you always need to think about every situation you are getting yourself into. Remember to never-never go off with anyone, unless you directly ask your parents first.

"Most of the people you know are good. Probably all of the people you know and will meet in your lifetime would never hurt children. But that doesn't mean you should take any chances by getting into a car, or going into a home, without hearing your parents tell you directly that it's ok.

"Instead of getting into that man's car with him, I should have ridden my bike, as fast as I could, home to see for myself if my mom was gone.

13/ PICK-UP-PASSWORD

"It can be confusing because it is possible that an unplanned situation may come up when your parents do need someone to pick you up without them being able to tell you first. It would be a good idea to talk to your mom and dad when you get home and come up with a Pick-Up-Password.

"If there is ever an emergency and your parents unexpectedly need to have someone get you, that person would have to tell you the Pick-Up-Password before you got into his or her car or went into their house. When someone tells you the password, you would know that the person really did talk to your parents.

"Just remember; NEVER tell your Pick-Up-Password to anyone! Make sure you always keep your password a family secret. If you do tell someone your password, then it is not safe anymore. Do not tell it to your best friends. Do not tell it to your uncle. Do not even tell it to your dog, (in case someone hears you say it.) It is your job to know the word, not to say the word. Actually, don't even tell people that you have a Pick-Up-Password and then you will be less tempted to say what it is.

"Your mom or dad should be the only one who gives away your family's Pick-Up-Password. It might also be a good idea to change the password every so often. You and your family can figure out all the details to the Pick-Up-Password, but you should definitely use one."

Wow. I couldn't believe all that Cindy had just told us. I felt so sad for her. I also grieved for the little boy, and his family, who Cindy was telling us about. How many children have been tricked and hurt or had their lives stolen from them? I didn't want to think about what it must have been like for Cindy to be kidnapped and hurt.

I still had tears running down my face from listening to her story. Even though she explained why she told us, I wondered why it was us that she had to help. Why was she telling us to be careful? It is true, we have left Mom a few times when we were at carnivals or other crowded fun places. But we have never had a guy, woman, or teenager try to kidnap us. I don't think we have even really had a stranger try to talk to us.

Oh, wait… one time a man was walking his dog down our Aunt Kellie's street. Sylvia and I were playing outside while my mom and Aunt Kellie were inside. We wanted to pet the dog, so we asked him if we could.

While we were petting his dog, he talked to us; he was asking us questions about stuff we liked to do and eat. Later, one of Aunt Kellie's neighbors told Mom that she saw us talking to a guy whom she didn't recognize. Mom got really upset because we were talking to a stranger while there were no other adults around who we knew.

At the time, I didn't see the big deal. We were just petting his dog. But Mom was furious. She said she was scared, but she was acting mad, if you ask me. Now, after hearing Cindy's story, I think maybe Mom was so upset because she really did get scared about losing us.

It's all so very confusing. Mom says don't talk to strangers, yet she says it's never ok to pet a dog unless you ask the owner's permission first. Isn't that talking to a stranger? I guess, to be safe, we just stay away from all dogs and people unless our mom, neighbors, or other adults we know are outside with us.

"I see how it would be very easy to be tricked by an adult. We are always told we must do what adults tell us to do. Yet, we are also told there are some things we should never do even if an adult tells us to do it. Cindy, I understand how you made the mistake of getting into that man's car. I'm so sorry that happened to you." Even though I was trying to hold them back, tears escaped down my face, again.

"Thank you, Michaela, that was kind of you to say. Now, I am just glad that I was here to remind you. I know you are confused about how I am actually helping you, but you will understand soon enough. There will be a time in your near future that you will think of me and what happened to me, and you will remember that it is not ok to trust everyone.

"If a car ever pulls up close to you, make sure you back up a few feet. If the person in that car rolls down his or her window, or the window is already rolled down, take even more steps back away from the car. If the person or people in the car ask you for help or ask if you want a ride, scream NO and run away fast. Or if that person doesn't say anything but just starts to get out of the car RUN as fast as you can to the closest adult you know.

"If you are ever in a store, at a function, like a school carnival, a fair, a park, or play place and a stranger tries to talk to you, or you get separated from your parents, if it's possible, only ask help from a person who works at the place where you are. You can bet that an employee is a safe person to ask for help. If you can't find a person who is working, then try to find someone that looks like a mom and has her kids with her. You can also bet a mom with kids is a safe person to speak to. Do you both understand?"

We smiled at her and told her we thought we understood.

As I was standing there, I made a promise to myself that I would never get into a car with someone I didn't know. If a stranger were ever to try to get me, I would run! Run far and run fast, and then tell Mom or Dad about it.

I didn't want to think about strangers and danger anymore. I just wanted to go home. I was starving! Then I remembered our HORSE basketball game. I asked Cindy if we still had to finish the game before we could go home.

She told us we didn't need to finish HORSE anymore. She told me the only thing I had to do before I was ready to go home was tie my shoe. Oh my gosh, my shoe was still untied! I bent down and tied it tight in a double knot. Then Cindy told us we were ready to go home.

"How do we get home?" Sylvia asked.

Cindy giggled and told us that we simply had to wake up. She reminded us that because we hit our heads so hard on the walls, we were really still unconscious up in her old room knocked out. All we had to do was figure out how to wake ourselves up.

I had an idea; I asked Cindy if we could have a couple buckets of cold water. As soon as I finished asking, the buckets appeared at our feet. As I picked up my bucket, I told Sylvia to pick up her bucket. I explained that my plan was to count to three and then we would each pour the buckets over our heads. If cold water didn't wake us up, I didn't know what would.

"One,   two,   three!"

14/ LESSON LEARNED

Sylvia and I were both on the old bedroom floor, slowly sitting up and rubbing our heads when I remembered everything that had happened. "Oh my gosh! Sylvia, are you ok?"

She said she was ok, but the back of her head had a big bump on it and hurt. I had the same bump on the back of my head too. However at that moment, I didn't care. Instead, I shrieked to Sylvia that we could go home!

We both stood up and looked at the rocking horse. While looking at it, I got a few tears in my eyes because the rocking horse made me think of Cindy. I was going to miss her. I hoped that she was finally with her family. The thought of her being with her family put a smile on my face, and I no longer felt so sad.

"Do you think we could take the rocking horse home?" Sylvia was looking at me with wide eyes.

"I don't think so. How would we explain it to Mom? Besides, it's the only thing Cindy has left. We can't take it from her."

"Oh yeah, I guess. I didn't think of it that way. I really like it and want something to remind me of this afternoon. Ya know?"

"Yeah I get it, Sylvia. We will just have to remind each other. We should never forget. For our sake and for Cindy and all the other children that have ever been hurt, we will remember."

We walked out of the bedroom and down the large dirty staircase and then out the front door of Cindy's old house. As we were leaving, I had a feeling we would be back there soon.

We were not sure which way was home, so we just started walking through the woods in as straight of a line as we could. Eventually, we came to a side street that we recognized as being near our house. All we had to do was walk down that street a little ways, and then we would be able to cross through a couple of our neighbors' yards. That would bring us to our own backyard.

Sylvia hadn't said much since we left. I wondered if she was thinking about Cindy. I was about to ask her what she was thinking, when I noticed a car driving down the street toward us. For some reason, the hairs on the back of my neck stood up. That sure did happen a lot on that day.

I told Sylvia that we should get out of the road and onto the other side of the ditch, to give the car enough room to drive by. She must have been nervous too because she didn't argue with me that there was plenty of room on the road for both the car and us. By the time we got a few feet into the field, the car was slowing down. It stopped in the road directly across from where we were standing. Sylvia and I just stood there looking at the car.

Then I remembered Cindy telling us if a car ever stopped near us to move back a couple feet. Even though we were on the other side of the ditch, I still felt we should back up a little more since the car had stopped. I grabbed Sylvia's hand and gave it a little tug to silently remind her that we needed to take a few steps back.

The driver was a man. There was also a woman in the car. They were smiling over at us. I could not remember ever seeing them before.

"Hey there young ladies, have you seen a dog running down this street or anywhere around here? Our dog just escaped out of the backyard, so we are driving around looking for her. We live right down there on the next street over," the man finished explaining by pointing toward a side street behind him.

I know I wasn't supposed to talk to him, but he was in his car so he wouldn't have been able to make us get in before we could start running. I just wanted him to drive away, so I told him we had not seen any dogs.

Then he explained to us that he had the missing dog's puppy in the car with them, and, if we wanted, we could take a look at the puppy because it looks just like the dog that ran away. That way we would know to call him if we ever see the dog running around our yard or street.

As soon as he got done talking, he opened his car door and started crawling out. Sylvia and I looked at each other and screamed, "NOOOO!" We ran as fast as we could. We ran through the field, across our neighbors' yards and then into our own without even looking back. We ran straight into our house and cried for Mom.

15/ BELIEVE

Mom came running into the room and yelled, "There you are! Where have you been? I told you to stay in the backyard, but I couldn't find you anywhere! I have been looking for the past 20 minutes!"

In between sobs we told her we got lost in the woods and about the people in the car. Mom got really upset and gave us a hug. She said they probably were looking for a dog, but we were very smart to get out of the street when the car drove up. And we were wise to run when he started getting out of the car. Mom said she was going to call the police to tell them about the man and woman because they sounded a little suspicious to her.

She asked us what color was their car and how many doors it had. She also asked us to describe what the man and woman looked like. Mom asked if we noticed the letters and numbers on the license plate, but I told her that I didn't take the time to look. After we answered all her questions, she told us to go wash up while she called the police, and then we could have dinner.

Dinner! Oh boy! I can't even begin to tell you how hungry I was. I could have eaten a horse! A horse… oh, that made me think of Cindy again.

In the bathroom, while we were washing our hands, I asked Sylvia if we should tell Mom about Cindy, her house, and the rocking horse. Sylvia thought we shouldn't because she didn't think Mom would believe us. Sylvia didn't even know if *she* believed it all really happened. I had to agree. It was all so unreal; we should just keep that story to ourselves.

Like my tree Kasidy keeps all her stories and secrets to herself by storing them inside her leaves, Sylvia and I should keep Cindy to ourselves, storing her inside our memories. I thought to myself that maybe someday I would let my brain tell my fingers the memories of

Cindy. Then my fingers could tell a pen and the pen could then write the story on paper.

Well, that someday had come because I felt that it was time to share this with you. That's why you are reading this. Cindy told us her story in hopes of helping us. And, I think she succeeded. And now, I'm telling you her story in hopes of helping you. Hopefully, you will never have to think about what to do if a stranger tries to take you. But if you do, you can remember this story and RUN! You can learn from Cindy's mistake, just like Sylvia and I did.

After dinner that night, Sylvia and I went into our room and watched TV. We didn't talk much, even though I had a lot on my mind, as I am sure Sylvia did. However before we fell asleep, I asked her if she still didn't know whether or not to believe it all actually happened.

Up until that day, I believed that ghosts didn't exist. Sylvia and I ended up agreeing that it was much easier to believe in Cindy and her story than it was to believe that we both got knocked out and had the same dream. Still, either way, it was hard to believe.

I still needed to talk to Mom and Dad about a Pick-Up-Password. I didn't ever want to let myself get tricked by anyone. I want to live a long and happy life with my sister and the rest of my family. I was so thankful for my bed, my sister, in her bed next to mine, my mom and dad, my baby brother, and dinner... everything! That night, I fell asleep with a smile on my face.

The next morning while we were eating breakfast, Mom told us that an abandoned house down the road had burned down in the middle of the night. Sylvia and I looked at each other, and I could tell she was thinking the same thing I was thinking; Cindy's house! Mom asked us if we wanted to take a walk after Jonathan's nap to look at the burned down house.

We both told Mom that we really wanted to see it. Sylvia asked if we could go right then. Mom insisted that we wait until after Jonathan's nap. She explained that after his nap, we would put him in his stroller and walk through the neighbor's yard to the side street. That street would take us right by the house that burned down.

That sounded exactly like the way we came back from Cindy's house. Sylvia and I were so excited we could hardly stand the wait. Jeesh, Jonathan's naps were always getting in our way.

It was finally time to go for our walk! Mom decided to bring her camera so she could take pictures of the burned rubble. Mom loves to take pictures of abandoned houses. She told us that she was actually taking pictures at that house just the other day. She was curious to see what kind of pictures she would get since it had burned.

Oh wow! Mom had already been to Cindy's house! I didn't know that. "Hey Mom, did you get a picture of the..." Oops! I cut myself off because I was going to ask about the rocking horse in Cindy's bedroom! How would I have explained to her that I knew about that!?

"Did I get a picture of the what?" she questioned.

I quickly replied that I was wondering if she got a picture of the inside of the house so that Sylvia and I could see what it looked like before it burned. Whew... that was a close call.

I could see Sylvia giving me a dirty look that warned 'you almost blew it sister!'

Mom set Jonathan in his stroller and we walked to the house. Sylvia and I couldn't believe our eyes! It was definitely Cindy's house. It was hard to believe that the house we were in just the day before was almost completely gone. Only one wall was left standing and it was very burned. There were burned boards, nails, dishes, books and all sorts of rubble around the house.

There was also a burned piano in the middle of the remains. I told Sylvia I didn't remember seeing a piano, and she said she didn't either. Our mom asked us what we were talking about. We looked at each other, and then I explained to Mom that I had never seen a burned piano before, and Sylvia said she hadn't either. Whew! That was another close call.

I got tears in my eyes because we were standing in front of what used to be Cindy's house, and it had been reduced to a pile of charred wood and junk. I was wondering where Cindy might be, as I looked at the big burned pile of her memories spread out in front of me.

Slowly, I walked around and studied everything. My eyes kept wandering back to the piano. I stepped over a few boards so that I could get closer. Sylvia was walking toward me; I guess she wanted to know what I was investigating.

When I got a few steps closer to the piano, I saw a burned picture frame. I could tell the picture inside the frame was not burned. Maybe the glass protected it from the fire. I picked it up and wiped the dark soot off the glass, so I could see the picture better.

There she was! Cindy was smiling up at me from inside the picture! I showed Sylvia what I had found. Cindy was sitting on the front steps of her house with her family, and they were all smiling. It was the best treasure ever! Sylvia and I were both right yesterday; we ended up finding a ghost and a little piece of treasure in that great big house that I was almost too chicken to go in.

Sylvia said, "I think Cindy is with her family now. I bet that is why the house burned down. Maybe since she was finally able to leave, she didn't want anyone else to rock on her rocking horse or go through her house. Perhaps she burned it down when she left."

All I could say was, "I think you are right, Sylvia. Cindy must be with her family now."

I know this might sound crazy, but it looked like Cindy winked up at us after I finished agreeing with Sylvia. Sylvia must have seen it also because she got a huge grin on her face. I took the picture out of the burned frame and put it in the bottom of Jonathan's stroller, so we could take it home and keep it forever.

Mom asked us to walk over near her because she wanted to take a photo of us next to the burned down house. If she only knew just how much that house really meant to Sylvia and me, she would have understood how happy we were to have her take our picture next to it. We would always have the pictures to remind us of Cindy, her stories, and lessons.

ABOUT THE AUTHOR

Karrie Loomis grew up in Mason, Michigan. She joined the Navy when she was 18 and served for six years. Three years after being honorably discharged, she graduated from Old Dominion University, earning a B.A.S. in psychology, minoring in religious studies.

Karrie currently lives in Virginia Beach, Virginia with her three children. She enjoys writing, reading, photography, and spending time at the beach.

The Rocking Horse was written by Karrie for her children. This book is an elaborated version of a story she made up and told her kids one morning while driving them to school. It is one of the ways she has tried to instill on her children to never get into a car with strangers.

Karrie hopes that, through this book, she can reach out to many children, reminding them to never get into a car with strangers.

The Rocking Horse is Karrie's first published book.

To get in contact with the author, you may email her at: karrieloomis@yahoo.com.